www.mascotbooks.com

Mirth Meets Earth

For more information, please contact:
Mascot Books
620 Herndon Parkway #320
Herndon, VA 20170
info@mascotbooks.com

Library of Congress Control Number: 2018902032

CPSIA Code: PRT0818A
ISBN-13: 978-1-68401-459-0

Printed in the United States

MIRTH
MEETS
EARTH

Discover the continents with a most curious space pup

written by Michelle Glasser

illustrated by Jaclyn Stein

Greetings, Earthlings!
Mirth is my name, and traveling space is my game.

I may have a puppy dog face,
but I am a furry explorer from deep in space.

I love to sniff out treasures, friends,
and adventures that never end.

I've already dug around the galaxy,
but your planet is the next place I want to see.

Wow! There she is, shining bright in the sun's light.
Earth and her moon are a beautiful sight.

Colorful and round like a ball at the beach,
Earth spins constantly, even while you sleep.

Did you know your planet orbits the sun once a year?
To learn more I must enter your atmosphere!

As gravity quickens my motion,
I see cotton white clouds and the world's blue oceans.

Today, I'm interested in the green part—the land—
seven continents as rich as they are grand.

They hold billions of people just like you,
each with their own body, mind, and thoughts, too.

Earth's continents are full of life and wonder,
from the North Pole to Australia, way down under.

Africa, Asia, Australia, Antarctica, Europe, and the Americas, South and North...
Let's turn the page and venture forth!

Africa's many countries have lots of terrains:
jungle, desert, mountains, and savannahs, such as the great Serengeti plain.

There are busy cities to see, like Casablanca and Lagos, to name a few.
We can even climb Cape Town's Table Mountain for a most amazing view.

Let's go on safari to meet wildlife mile after mile;
or to Egypt to check out the pyramids and the River Nile.

With vibrant cultures and beautiful beasts,
Africa holds lots of adventures and people to meet.

ANTARCTICA

Off to the bottom of the globe, we roll.
Antarctica is what many call the South Pole!

If braving extreme temperatures is your wish,
we can hang out with penguins, seals, and local ice fish!

Cold and windy with a whole lot of space,
there are many adventures to be had in this place.

A glacial wonderland that's frozen and remote,
Antarctica can only be visited by plane or by boat.

From Vietnam to Russia,
Armenia to Japan,
Asia has the most people
of all the lands.

The Great Wall of China
is not to be missed.
Let's explore its
thousands of miles,
every curve and twist.

We can climb the Himalayas up in Nepal,
then cool down under Bali's Munduk Waterfall.

Did you know that behind India's Taj Mahal is an old love story?
Today, let's marvel at it in all its glory.

Curious pups like me love Asia because there's much to inspect,
like Turkey's Bosphorus Bridge, where two continents connect!

Jordan's ancient city of Petra is a sight to behold.
Carved from sandstone, it still dazzles in rose gold.

The Middle East is home to Mesopotamia, where it all began.
It's now Syria, Iraq, Kuwait, and Iran.

Millions of Earthlings come each year to have a look.
Let's check out Israel's Sea of Galilee and taste the flavors of the Shuk.

Australia is part of the Oceania region,
made up of islands that form an important legion.

One continent and one country that's shaped like a leaf,
let's discover Australia's cities, the Outback, and the Great Barrier Reef.

Only here can we play with
   koalas and kangaroos
and other animals the rest of the
   world can only see at zoos.

Many Australians came from
   faraway nations,
but it also has a diverse native
   foundation.

In Europe, the people of over fifty countries live side by side.
Here we can ski the great Alps and take a cog ride.

With modern cities that go back thousands of years,
ancient sites can be found with every turn and steer.

Europe has the Netherlands, where they grow almost every flower,
Britain's Big Ben, and France's Eiffel Tower.

From Scotland to Poland, Finland to Spain,
Europe's treasures can be seen by boat, plane, and mostly by train.

Across the ocean, there's Canada, Central America, and the USA.
North America reaches from the top of the globe to Earth's midway.

Let's harvest grains in the Great Plains, swim in the tropical sun,
and head north for some hockey fun.

With cities that have skylines that light up the night,
the buildings of Chicago and New York reach great heights.

Some once believed this land was discovered a few hundred years ago,
but native people have lived here since ancient times, most now know.

Migrating to South America with a friendly flock of birds,
this continent offers many places to uncover, I've heard.

Let's meet animals on Ecuador's Galapagos Islands and climb Peru's Machu Picchu.
We can even dance the tango in Argentina, too!

South America has the longest mountain range, the Andes that soar; here we can also take incredible Patagonian tours.

The Amazon rainforest is fun to observe, but it may hold the key to life that can only be unlocked if it's conserved.

Wow! That was a whirlwind of a trip.
And there's so much more we mustn't skip!

I will return soon so we can sniff around Earth together.
This definitely isn't goodbye forever.

You all share a beautiful home;
one that connects each Earthling, a planet to care for and roam.

Until the next time,

Mirth

A most curious space pup

ABOUT THE AUTHOR

Born and bred in New Jersey, Michelle Glasser spent her professional life as a healthcare copywriter for big New York City advertising agencies after graduating from Rutgers University. It was her two curious toddler boys, who were eager to learn about the globe in their father's office, that sparked the Mirth Meets Earth fantasy. Motherhood also inspired Michelle to design products that make life easier. You can find her award-winning leash for terrestrial-traveling dogs and other unique pet products at sitstaygoco.com. Michelle lives with her family in northern New Jersey, along with their rescue pup, Snoopy, who recently came from Puerto Rico.

ABOUT THE ILLUSTRATOR

Jaclyn Stein was born in Montreal, Quebec, Canada, so it's no surprise that a whole page of this book is dedicated to Mirth learning hockey in North America. While she is currently a creative director for two jewelry brands, Jaclyn's childhood fantasy was to illustrate children's books, so the release of this one is a dream come true for her. A proud Canadian with a degree from McGill University, Jaclyn is currently living the American dream in New York with her husband and three young children.